Best Day
of the Week

by Nancy Carlsson-Paige
with illustrations by Celeste Henriquez

Redleaf Press

© 1998 Nancy Carlsson-Paige
Illustrations by Celeste Henriquez

Published by: Redleaf Press
                 a division of Resources for Child Caring
                 450 N. Syndicate, Suite 5
                 St. Paul, MN 55104-4125

Library of Congress Cataloging-in-Publication Data

Carlsson-Paige, Nancy.
    Best day of the week / by Nancy Carlsson-Paige ;
illustrations by Celeste Henriquez.
            p.   cm.
    Summary: Because Calvin wants to play pirates and Angela wants to
play store with an old card table which they found in the trash,
they must find a way to resolve their conflict.
    ISBN 1-884834-52-3
    [1. Conflict (Psychology)—Fiction.   2. Problem solving—Fiction.]
I. Henriquez, Celeste, ill. II. Title.
PZ7.C216835Be   1998
[E] — dc21   98-14401
                                                          CIP
                                                           AC

For Kyle and Matt
who have always known where to find the hidden treasure

Calvin woke up when he heard his brother cough in the crib next to him. Their bedroom was still dark, but Calvin could tell by the noises outside on the street that it was morning.

Calvin felt tired. He didn't want to get up. Then he remembered what day it was. Thursday. The best day of the week.

The day everyone in the neighborhood put out their trash.

The day that people put things they didn't want anymore out on the sidewalk for the city trucks to pick up.

The day Calvin might find something interesting to play with among the things people threw away.

Like the old broken table leg he was using for a telescope when he played pirates.

And the box full of Styrofoam pieces that Calvin and Angela pretended were pirates' treasure.

Angela lived in the apartment next door to Calvin.
She was his best friend.

Every morning Angela and Calvin walked to school with Angela's big brother Hector.

Hector was forever saying to Angela and Calvin, "Hurry up. Walk faster or we'll be late to school."

But on Thursdays, Hector always made sure they left a little early so there would be time to look over the trash.

As they left Calvin's house this Thursday morning, Calvin's mother walked with them to the front steps. "You can look at the things thrown away on the street," she said, "but don't you go pokin' around inside any trash bags. You understand?"

Three heads nodded up and down. Calvin and Hector nodded slowly. Angela's head moved twice as fast. Calvin's mother smiled. "Have a wonderful day," she said.

The friends headed toward school but didn't spot anything very interesting for three blocks.

Then, as they rounded the corner onto Center Street, Angela stopped and pointed.

A square object stood between two trash barrels in front of a brick building.

Getting closer, they realized that the square object was a folded card table—with only one leg bent and just a few scrapes on the top.

Angela examined the table, then announced, "We can play with this after school!"

"How are we going to keep it until then?" Calvin asked. But Hector was already pulling the table out from between the two barrels.

Hector guided the card table toward a narrow space between two buildings. Then they all pushed the table into the alleyway.

Hector gave the table an extra nudge to get it fully out of view.

All day in school Calvin thought about the card table.
He thought about how he could throw a blanket over it and
make it into a perfect pirates' cave.

Angela thought about the card table all day too.
She thought about how she could put a blanket over it and
make it into a perfect place to play store.

Calvin thought, "I'll hide in the pirates' cave and spy
on the bad pirates."

Angela thought, "I'll get some paper and scissors and make
signs to put in my store."

Hector, Angela, and Calvin nearly ran out of school to the spot where they'd hidden the card table. Three pairs of eyes peered into the dark alley. The card table leaned against the brick wall. Exactly as they had left it.

Angela and Calvin dragged the table into Calvin's apartment and into his room. They called out the window to Hector, "We got it to stand up!" Hector waved to them as he walked down the street to meet the big kids.

Angela and Calvin got a blanket and threw it over the top of the table.
They peered into the dark space underneath.
It was all closed up.
A perfect place to play.

Then, at the exact same moment, Calvin and Angela both spoke:

"Let's get the pirate treasure and play pirates," said Calvin.
"Let's put all kinds of stuff in it and play store," said Angela.

Calvin looked at Angela.
Angela looked at Calvin.

"You always want to play store," Calvin said. "Let's play pirates."

"Pirates is all you ever want to play," said Angela. "I want to play store."

Calvin's eyes got sharp. "But there are no bad guys in store," he said. "It's a dumb game."

Angela's eyes got dark. "Well, pirates isn't fun for me," she said. "It's a stupid game."

Calvin's mouth got small and thin. He said, "Store is a stupid girls' game. And you're a stupid girl."

Angela felt her face get hot.

She opened her mouth. She wanted to tell Calvin that he was a dumb and stupid boy. But she stopped.

She looked at Calvin.
She could still hear Calvin's mean words.

Angela felt hurt.
She was quiet.

Then Angela said, "I don't like it when you call me a stupid girl."

Calvin looked at Angela.
Her face was sad.

Calvin felt confused.

He was still mad, but he felt bad too.
And he still wanted to play pirates.

Calvin said, "I'll let you use my telescope if you'll play pirates."

Angela shook her head no.

Calvin tried another idea: "Why don't we play pirates first and then play store after that?"

Angela didn't want to play pirates first.
"We could play store first and then play pirates later," she said.

Calvin made a nasty face.

ngela looked away into the dark cozy space under the table. Right at that moment an idea burst into her mind. "I know what," she said. "We can play store and the pirates can come to the store and buy all the stuff they need for their ship!"

Calvin's brown eyes widened. "You mean we have the pirates come to the store?"
A grin spread across his face.

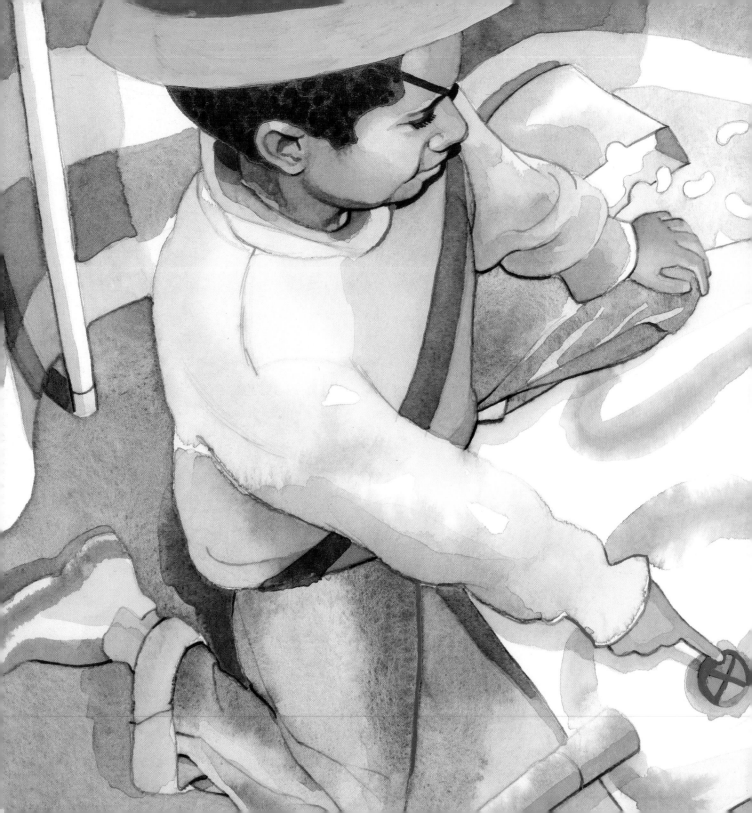

Calvin ran for the box of Styrofoam pieces he was using for pirate treasure. "The pirates can use this for money," he said. "Just the good pirates, though. We'll hide it from the bad pirates."

Angela grabbed paper from her school bag and began drawing a map. She drew lines and added some circles and put X's inside them. She handed her map to Calvin.

"Yes!" shouted Calvin. "This is how the pirates can find our store!"

This book raises questions regarding themes and issues that are of special importance in the lives of children growing up today. Themes such as conflict, gender, and "bad guys" will resonate deeply with many children and provide a vehicle for adults to:

- Help children learn to solve their conflicts without violence.
- Help girls and boys learn to play together.
- Help children develop their imaginative play and use creative play materials.
- Help children learn to play "bad guy" themes in ways that are safe and allow them to work out their own developmental needs.

For information about how to use this book to help children work on these issues, see *Before Push Comes to Shove: Building Conflict Resolution Skills with Children* by Nancy Carlsson-Paige and Diane E. Levin (St. Paul: Redleaf Press, 1998).

Also from Redleaf Press

All the Colors We Are: The Story of How We Get Our Skin Color - Outstanding full-color photographs showcase the beautiful diversity of human skin color and offers children a simple, accurate explanation of how we are the color we are. Bilingual English/Spanish.

For the Love of Children: Daily Affirmations for People Who Care for Children - An empowering book filled with quotes, stories, and affirmations for each day of the year.

The Kindness Curriculum - Over 60 imaginative, exuberant activities that create opportunities for kids to practice kindness, empathy, conflict resolution, respect, and more.

Making It Better: Activities for Children Living in a Stressful World - This important book offers bold new information about the physical and emotional effects of stress, trauma, and violence on children today and gives teachers and caregivers the confidence to help children survive, thrive, and learn.

Reflecting Children's Lives - A practical guide to help you put children and childhood at the center of your curriculum. Rethink and refresh your ideas about scheduling, observations, play, materials, space, and emergent themes.

Roots and Wings: Affirming Culture in Early Childhood Programs - A unique approach to multicultural education that helps shape positive attitudes toward cultural differences.

Those Icky Sticky Smelly Cavity-Causing but...Invisible Germs - This is an imaginative tool to help children develop good toothbrushing habits. Bilingual English/Spanish.

Those Itsy-Bitsy Teeny-Tiny Not-So-Nice Head Lice - Teaches children and adults about how head lice are spread, commonly used methods for getting rid of lice, and ways to prevent the spread and reinfestation of head lice. Bilingual English/Spanish.

Those Mean Nasty Dirty Downright Disgusting but...Invisible Germs - This popular children's book shows the five germ characters that cause illness. Teach children the importance of hand washing. Bilingual English/Spanish.

1-800-423-8309